THE GIFT

For Angela and Natalie, with my love —JK

For Patti —PP

Text © 1995 by Joseph Kertes
Illustrations © 1995 by Peter Perko
Reprinted 1996

Groundwood Books / Douglas & McIntyre Ltd.
585 Bloor Street West, Toronto, Ontario M6G 1K5

Distributed in the U.S. by Publishers Group West
4065 Hollis Street, Emeryville CA 94608

The publisher gratefully acknowledges the assistance of the Canada Council
and the Ontario Arts Council.

Canadian Cataloguing in Publication Data

Kertes, Joseph, 1951-
The gift

ISBN 0-88899-235-1

I. Perko, Peter. II. Title.

PS8571.E77G5 1995   jC813'.54   C95-930222-0
PZ7.K47Gi 1995

The illustrations are done in pen and ink, graphite pencil and coloured pencils
Book design by Michael Solomon
Printed in Hong Kong by Everbest Printing Co. Ltd.

The GIFT

Joseph Kertes

ILLUSTRATIONS BY

PETER PERKO

A Groundwood Book

DOUGLAS & McINTYRE

TORONTO / VANCOUVER / BUFFALO

I'LL always remember the Christmas of 1959. My family and I had come from Hungary just a few years before. We had left a war behind us and settled on an old, shady street near Bloor and Bathurst Streets in Toronto, a couple of blocks away from Honest Ed's discount department store.

There were many other newcomers in our neighbourhood: others from Hungary, some from Poland, some from the Ukraine, a few from Germany, and one family from Finland. And the one thing most of us had in common was that we wanted to be British-Canadian. We children wanted our parents to sound like Larry Wilson's parents, who were so confident and successful in the drug store they ran and who ate sausages with their eggs for breakfast, or Norma McIntyre's parents, who once scolded our teacher for keeping Norma late after school, or Brent Timmons' parents, both of whom ran for City Council and won.

I wanted to be British-Canadian so badly I once wrote to the queen on Victoria Day to congratulate her on her great-great-aunt's birthday, *and* I got an answer from Buckingham Palace with a red wax seal on the back! The letter, addressed to "Master Jacob Beck," was written by Susan White, the queen's lady-in-waiting, and it said that Her Majesty had appreciated my kind words and wished me well in my school year. For two months I carried that letter with me everywhere I went, until the wax seal began to soften into a blob, and I got scared and carefully put away the letter in a box.

But what I wanted to be besides British-Canadian—and what most of the other new Canadians already were—was Christian.

The reason for my longing was Christmas. Christmas was bigger than anything else in the year, bigger than life itself. When Christmas approached, there was no December, no hockey, no Canada, no

The Gift

"Duke of Earl." There was only Christmas. It was so big and warm and glistening, it squeezed out all of life's other events. People sang songs about it and brought home fragrant trees and decorated them and wrapped presents and baked cookies and sang some more and sucked on pepperminty candy canes and watched out for Santa and sent wish-lists to Santa and felt sorry for Rudolph and tumbled with Jack Frost.

After the holidays, my classmates, with "Jingle Bells" and cookies still on their breaths, asked, "What-did-you-get-what-did-you-get-what-did-you-get?" and I always had ready a short list of things I could lie about: "A pair of pajamas, a hockey stick and six boxes of chocolate which I ate in one day and got sick."

And still, though it was January, at the front in the corner like an angel beside the teacher's desk was the little hero of the holidays: a baby Jesus doll in a manger with his parents and the three wise men—and above our heads, near the P.A. box and beside the portrait of the radiant queen was the picture of the grown-up Jesus, having his last supper, patiently awaiting Easter.

We recited the Lord's Prayer with the principal over the P.A. and sang "God Save the Queen" accompanied by the tinny music coming out of that box above our heads. Then we settled in and started the day with English. Our teacher asked us to write a composition called "Our Christmas Holidays."

The Gift

Christmas was not bright at our house, but grey. Except when my brother Noah and I watched shows about miracles on 34th Street and elsewhere or gazed into the silver eyes of the Ghost of Christmas Future. We did not deck the halls. No Christmas tree twinkled in our living room. No lights from our porch winked out at the feathery snow. We had no Santa, no gifts, no mangers. Our voices did not "Hark, the Herald" along with the angels. We did not steal extra minutes to listen for hooves and sleigh bells on our roof nor for the creaking of black boots on our living room floor.

Instead, our mother baked us strudel— apple for Noah and poppyseed for me— and our father said we could stay up to

watch all of "The Wizard of Oz" even if we had to fight off sleep to see Dorothy reach the Emerald City.

For days, our parents told us we could not call our friends. We could not "disturb the sanctity of their homes," they said—whatever that meant. It was a holiday, they said, an important holiday like Yom Kippur and Passover, and a family time.

So Noah and I, on Christmas morning, would go out to the skating rink at the park around the corner from our house—the only morning of the year we could have the rink all to ourselves—and we would set up my boots as goal posts, and he would take shots at me—"Gordie Howe shoots—oh!—the Gumper gets his leg out in front of it. He shoots again. He scores!"—

14

and then I would take shots at him—
"Mahovlich shoots—oh!—Glen Hall smoth-
ers the puck!"

And then it happened. It was to be our
fourth Christmas in Canada. It was the
afternoon of December 24, 1959, and my
friend, Larry Wilson, called to invite me
over to his place for Christmas lunch the
next day.

Noah sat staring at me glumly from
across the kitchen table as I asked our
mother if I could go.

"But we're having guests ourselves
tomorrow," she said in Hungarian. "The
Virags are coming over to light the
Hanukkah candles. You know how much
fun you always have with Tommy."

"Oh, please, Mommy. It'll just be for a

15

little while, I promise."

"I don't know. I don't think it's right."

"Why don't you let him go?" Noah
said. "It's just this once. Let him go."

"Well, it will depend on what your
father has to say about it. He's gone out to
the bank and a few other places to drop off
some bottles of wine. Even if he says yes,
you'd still have to buy a present—you can't
go empty-handed—so I just don't know."

So I waited for my father by the big picture window looking out onto our street,
Howland Avenue. I waited and waited. At
two o'clock, I heard the bells of St. Alban's
across the way ring out the first notes of
"Silent Night." Then I heard them again at
three o'clock. I watched the light begin to
fail. I watched people crunching home in

clumpy rubber boots, cheerful and with packages. I saw a boy, younger than me, being pulled on a sleigh by an older sister with a long white scarf. I heard a crow caw from the top of the big, bare maple standing on our lawn, and I watched the lights on the porches come on: the Cwynars' lights all different colours, the Dobrianskys' lights all white, and the Oszolis' lights all light green but trailing off to fill their bushes so that they looked in the dark like fireflies.

Noah asked if I wanted to go skating, and when I said no, he put on one of the first three records we ever owned: "Chantilly Lace."

And then, finally, I saw my father from way up the street, trudging toward our house. I jumped to my feet, grabbed my coat, pulled on my boots and burst out the door. I fell twice—once right over a snow bank—before I reached my father, so I was covered with snow when I did.

"What's all the excitement?" he said, looking worn-out but happy.

He brushed snow out of my hair, and then I told him.

"But how can you go?" he said. "It's not really for us."

"Please, Dad, I want to go."

"I don't think so." He started walking again.

"Please, Dad, I *need* to go."

He turned and looked into my eyes. "You *need* to?"

I nodded.

He pulled off one of his gloves and reached into his pocket to pull out his wallet. "Then you'll need money, too, to buy a gift." He handed me a two-dollar bill. "Go, find something, and don't be late for dinner."

I kissed his cold cheek, then turned and ran. I shouted up into the falling snow! I ran all the way down to Bloor Street and joined the happy crowds, then along Bloor Street past Steven's Milk at Bathurst and past it toward Honest Ed's. I was panting as I rushed into the hot building and over the old, creaky floorboards from the transistor radio section, to the model airplanes, then upstairs to the hockey gloves and sweaters, none of which I could afford.

I left the store and turned the corner

down Bathurst. My chest filled with the spirit of the baby in the manger and the little drummer boy and Bing Crosby and the blessed star and the Scarecrow and Toto and the three wise men. I did not feel the time pass—I could have gone on for days—and *did* go on for over an hour until I got all the way down Queen Street to Simpson's.

And there before me were the windows!—the great big beautiful windows with the whirling bunnies and towering castles and pretty princesses and Pooh bears and Bambi and a figure skater spinning on a tiny pond and valleys and little hills and warm banks of snow sprinkled by fairies and angels circling in the heavens above. Oh, there had never been such win-

dows in all of the dreams of all of the people on this earth! Not anywhere! Not ever!

And here they were now, bursting with
enchantment—all for me—for me, too.

I whirled, and my hand was on the long
brass door handle. I pushed and it held.
Then I pulled. I turned to see the sign:

CLOSED UNTIL
BOXING DAY, 9:00 A.M.
MERRY CHRISTMAS AND
HAPPY NEW YEAR TO ALL OUR
VALUED CUSTOMERS.

I pulled again on the door, then kicked
it. I backed away and backed until I
backed into a fire hydrant down the street.
The magic windows now looked like

bright aquariums. I turned to see the build-
ings all up and down the street, dark and
closed for the holidays but festooned with
banners, wishing each and every one of us
a Merry Christmas, and to all a good
night.

I ran again all the way to Bathurst
Street and hopped aboard a streetcar
where I broke my two-dollar bill and,
huddling in a seat at the very back, tried to
catch my breath. Steam rose from my
hands.

I got off at Bloor and ran back to
Honest Ed's. Closed. Sammy's Fresh Fish.
Closed. Cora's Flowers, Bill's Smoke and
Gift, The Florida Café. Closed, Closed,
Closed.

And then I saw it: Steven just leaving

Steven's Milk and hunting for the key. I sprinted over like an Olympian. "Please, Mr. Steven, please, can you just wait one more minute until I get my friend a gift— just one more minute, please?"

"Well, I guess I can wait," he said.

(He was like us, my mother later told me, except his name was Mr. Pollock, not Mr. Steven, and Larry Wilson told me Mr. Pollock had had his phone number tattooed on his arm.)

I searched frantically up and down the three aisles of the bright little store. I picked up chocolates, put them back, picked up a pen and pencil set and put it back, picked up a comic book and put it back. I was dizzy again with the whirling of the elves, my ears filling with the siren

call of angels. I floated past the dozen plastic Elvis heads, past the three tall porcelain Lassies and stopped at last at the solitary plaster cast of "The Last Supper." The baby in the manger was grown. His face and the faces around him glowed. They beckoned.

"The Last Supper" cost me ninety-nine cents, *and* it came with its own box. I paid a dime for gold wrapping paper and left the store warmed by the belief that the best things can be found closest to home.

I would not let anyone open my box. I did not think that they would understand. I gave my father his change, and asked my mother, please, to wrap the box before Noah got into it. And as I went to sleep that night, the big white radiator ticking in the bedroom I shared with Noah, I still felt the warmth in my cheeks and thought it might have come from the treasure wrapped in gold, perched royally on my very own table.

The next day, my friend Larry welcomed me into his house with a big warm grin. The tree in the living room, under which he placed my gift, blazed with colour.

"I've got something for you, too," he said. "We'll open them after lunch."

But it took forever for lunch to get under way. I thought for a while that waiting was one part of the Christmas tradition I had not heard about. When we were finally called, I saw place cards for all of us at the dinner table. They were nestled on sprigs of evergreen. Mine said, "Mr. Jacob Beck," and it was printed like the envelope from Buckingham Palace.

Lunch was as big as a big dinner. We ate turkey with cranberry sauce, stuffing and sweet potatoes, then pudding and tarts and fruitcake with clumps of fruit like plastic. Larry's little sisters giggled all the way through the meal, and Mr. Wilson asked if my family was well and about my favourite subject in school, but nothing else at all. I let out a breath of relief when he and Mrs. Wilson then talked for a long time about their friends, the Morrisons, and about how Stan Morrison was laid up with his leg in a cast after he broke it skiing.

After lunch, Larry and I opened our

presents. The one for me was wrapped in reindeer paper and was much thinner and a bit longer than the one I'd given to Larry. When I opened my very first Christmas gift, my heart pounded. I didn't want to rip the paper, so I gingerly peeled back the tape until it gave, and then, finally, there it was! Three Classics Illustrated comic books: *Treasure Island, The Last of the Mohicans* and *Oliver Twist.*

I held them to my chest the way my aunts and uncles held me as I waited for Larry to open his. He wasn't as careful with the paper and tore the side of the box which my mother had taped so delicately. Then he pulled out the plaster cast of "The Last Supper."

"Oh," he said. "Thanks." And he laid it

down by his foot with a small thud. He looked down between his knees at nothing at all, so that I could not see his face. "I got a hockey net from Santa," he said, "and some goalie pads. Do you want to go out and take some shots at me?"

"You don't like what I got you?" I asked. I felt my cheeks burning. "I do—I really do—but maybe I should have got you the Classics Illustrated *Ten Commandments* or something. They had that, too."

Then he smiled—not warmly as before—but the smile at the beginning of a laugh.

I snatched up my coat and boots and bolted like a rabbit, scattering my comic books in the snow behind me. "Come back!" Larry called to me, but I was already a half block away. Darkness was already falling. I thanked heaven for the darkness already falling!

Larry was now at the end of his walk with just his boots on and still calling. "You're my best friend! I'm sorry! I don't care about stupid gifts or anything! Please come back!"

When I was a full block away, I stopped and turned. "Tomorrow," I said. "I'm sorry. Call me tomorrow!" And he, too, waved as I watched him bend to pick up my comics.

Tears poured down my face and burned my cold cheeks before cooling them. I felt helpless and angry and spun around and stopped one last time before turning the corner. Larry was gone now,

and there was not a soul to be seen out through the darkness and the falling snow.

At Kendal Park, just around the corner from our house, I saw a girl on the rink. She was dressed for ballet and seemed to spin and bound, spin and bound as if she were stirring the sprinkling snow.

What was she doing here on Christmas Day?

I drew closer and gazed at her long, magic legs as now, over and over, she drew sideways figure-eights with the bright blades of her skates between the straight, painted lines of our hockey rink.

I took a deep breath and walked on until I turned the corner onto Howland. I could already see our porch from the distance. I wiped my face on my cold coat

sleeve and straightened up as tall as I could.

Our window glowed yellow out onto the blue snow. I peered in before entering and saw Tommy and the Virags, then my big brother Noah and my sweet parents, gathering around our dining room table— all decked out in lace and silver and my mother's fine china—and I waited and watched as they lit the eight Hanukkah candles, signifying the end of the festival of lights.